This book belongs to

....

Copyright © 2014

make believe ideas ltd

The Wilderness, Berkhamsted, Hertfordshire, HP4 2AZ, UK.
501 Nelson Place, P.O. Box 141000, Nashville, TN 37214-1000, USA.

www.makebelieveideas.com

Written by Tim Bugbird.
Illustrated by Lara Ede.
Designed by Ellie Fahy.

Pippa

the
Pumpkin
Fairy

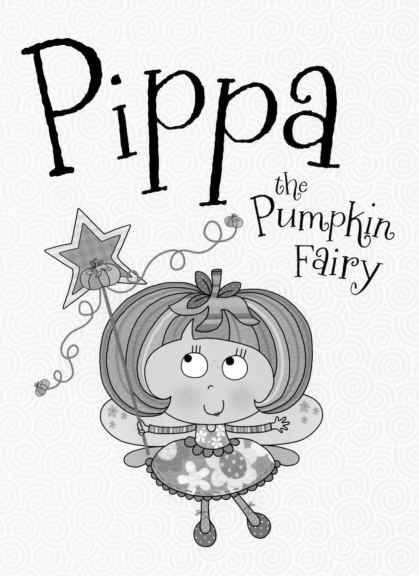

Tim Bugbird · Lara Ede

make
believe
ideas

When Pippa first used her fairy wand,
it was shiny, sparkly, and new.
One whoosh made a pumpkin lantern
and a swoosh made a face with a "BOO"!

The **lanterns** were made for a party
that came around once a year
when trees were turning **golden**
and **winter** was drawing near.

But, one year, Pippa was shocked —

when she waved her wand, she found

all the wrong kind of lanterns

in a row by her feet on the ground!

When Penny and Bea came over to see
how Pippa was getting along,
she panicked and covered the pumpkins.
"Great!" she said. "Nothing's wrong."

"The lanterns are just so BOO -ey,
I had to hide them away.

They're under this cloth so no one can see.

'Til the party, that's where they'll stay!"

"Promise," said Pippa, "you won't tell a soul.
We must not spoil the surprise."

But Penny and Bea **could not** resist

telling a **friend** or **two**.

The news was so **BIG**, and they didn't know

that what **Pippa** said wasn't **true**.

As Penny was talking, Pru overheard
and called Maisie (her very best friend),
who spread the word on Flitter –
Pippa's pumpkins began to trend!

BREAKING NEWS: Pippa's BOO-tiful pumpkins!

Talk of BOO-tiful pumpkins
soon made the national news.
And still Pippa's wand would not work —
she didn't know what to do!

The rumor was getting out of hand.
It was all a terrible mess.
But the longer she left it, the harder it was
for Pippa to try to confess!

The day of the pumpkin party arrived,
and the fairies couldn't wait to see
just how truly amazing
Pippa's lanterns were going to be.
Pippa nervously peeked outside,
watched by a TV crew.
"It's time at last!" the presenter announced.
"Pippa, over to you!"

Then, all of the sudden, out of the blue,
lightning cut through the sky.
The fairies looked up as the rain poured down –
they couldn't keep anything dry!

Decorations were **soggy**, and tables were wet;
the **cakes** and the snacks were soaked through.
The **party** was **ruined** — or so it seemed —
there was nothing the **fairies** could do!

Pippa thought, "It can't get **worse**;
I might as well come clean."

"I'm sorry," she said, "but I'm about to show
the WORST pumpkins you've ever seen."

There was a gasp, then stony silence, followed by laughter and cheers.

The fairies were **applauding** Pippa — she couldn't **believe** her ears!

Pippa's pumpkins weren't BOO – ey at all.

They didn't have "WOO"

or "WAA".

But with their funny-ha-ha faces,
they were the best-ever lanterns by far!

"We're **sorry** we started rumors," said Bea.

Pippa said, "I'm **sorry**, too.

I got into such a **muddle** —

I should have been **honest** with you."

The fairies put on their ponchos —
the rain wouldn't spoil their fun.

By the light of the laughing lanterns, their party had just begun!

Now, if ever you're in Fairy Land when leaves turn gold from green,

you'll find Pippa's pumpkin lanterns the FUNNIEST you've ever seen!